Welcome to the
incredible world of
the Night Zoo

Meet amazing
magical creatures!

Follow Will's
adventure as the
Night Zookeeper

Beware of the evil
army of Voids

Continue to explore
the Night Zoo at
nightzookeeper.com

HC

Meet the Characters

Will

The new Night Zookeeper, a force for good in a magical world that's under threat from an evil army of darkness.

Professor Penguin

A respected figure amongst the rebels of Igloo City, but can he be trusted?

Riya

Fast, brave, impulsive. She never lets a silly thing like rules stand in her way.

Sam

Extremely tall and extremely clumsy, but when it comes to spying, he's the best.

The Voids

Robotic spiders set on destroying the Night Zoo and plunging it into darkness.

This book was co-written by Giles Clare

OXFORD
UNIVERSITY PRESS

Great Clarendon Street, Oxford OX2 6DP

Oxford University Press is a department of the University of Oxford.
It furthers the University's objective of excellence in research, scholarship,
and education by publishing worldwide. Oxford is a registered trade mark of
Oxford University Press in the UK and in certain other countries

First published 2019

British Library Cataloguing in Publication Data
Data available

ISBN: 978-0-19-276407-2

1 3 5 7 9 10 8 6 4 2

Printed in Great Britain

Paper used in the production of this book is a natural,
recyclable product made from wood grown in sustainable forests.
The manufacturing process conforms to the environmental
regulations of the country of origin.

NIGHT ZOO KEEPER

The Penguins of Igloo City

Joshua Davidson

Illustrated by
Buzz Burman

OXFORD
UNIVERSITY PRESS

Chapter One

Will Rivers, the Night Zookeeper, stepped through the glowing portal, closely followed by his good friends Riya and Sam the Spying Giraffe. Will immediately raised his coat collar and tucked it closely around his neck: this new part of the Night Zoo was freezing cold. It couldn't have been more different from the pounding heat of the desert where they had just defeated the giant Void. Will moved forward carefully. The fresh snow creaked under each footstep.

'Be careful, guys,' he warned, his breath steaming in the crisp air. 'It's quite—'

Too late. Behind him, Sam's legs slid in four different directions. The young giraffe collapsed in a confused heap on the cold ground.

'—icy,' finished Will. 'You alright, Sam?'

Sam's chin was resting on the snow. He looked up at Will with his dark, masked eyes. 'Great Purple Elephants,' he said, his teeth chattering. 'This place is as slippery as a polished eel covered in soap!'

Riya, who was getting used to Sam's clumsiness, had nimbly leapt out of his way.

'Right, we seem to have entered a very different climate,' she announced. 'Look at all these buildings. They're all made of solid ice!'

Will examined their surroundings. There were domed houses everywhere, each carved from great blocks of ice. Flickering street lights

lit the narrow lanes between the igloos with a dull orange light. In the gloom, Will could also make out towering walls of ice beyond the rooftops. There was no movement, no welcome band, no celebration feast here. The streets were as quiet as the gently falling snow.

Sam rose to his feet and stared suspiciously at the ground. 'Hey, Riya,' he said. 'What's the difference between the weather and the climate?'

'Well, weather means—' began Riya, then stopped when she realized Sam was giving her a goofy smile. 'Oh no. Sam, this is one of your jokes, isn't it?' Sam nodded enthusiastically. Riya rolled her eyes. 'Go on, then. Spit it out, you long-necked camel,' she sighed. 'I don't know, Sam, what *is* the difference between

6

weather and climate?'

Sam grinned. 'Well, you can't weather a tree, but you can climate! Geddit? Climate? Climb it? Ha ha!'

Riya slapped her palm on her forehead and groaned.

'So I guess we're already inside Igloo City,' said Will. 'But where is everyone?' He swallowed as he was struck by a sudden fear. It was his job to protect the animals of the Night Zoo. He had just made a solemn promise to look after them. As Will looked around for signs of life, he wondered if he was too late. Had he failed to keep his promise already?

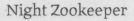

'Maybe the animals have fled,' suggested Riya. 'We should look for a gate in those city walls and follow them.'

'Hang on a minute! My ossicones are tingling,' said Sam.

'What is it, Sam?' asked Will urgently. 'There's a Void here, isn't there? I knew it! We're too late.'

Sam furrowed his brow. 'No, that's not it,' he said. 'I'm picking something else up. It's not danger as such. More something not quite

8

right. Something fishy.'

'Is it a fish?' suggested Riya unhelpfully.

'No, silly,' Sam replied. 'Fishy. You know, something suspicious.'

'Which way, Sam?' asked Will.

Using his spy senses to guide them, Sam led Will and Riya zigzagging through the narrow lanes. Perhaps it was the cold, but Will's injured leg was aching again. As they passed each dim streetlight, Will thought that they shone a little brighter, like someone blowing on the glowing embers of a fire.

'Look at this, Will,' said Riya. She was pointing at a black-and-white poster nailed to an igloo with jagged shards of ice. It read:

Residents of Igloo City, **YOU MUST NOT:**

- Paint (especially bright colours)
- Tell stories (Happy Ever Afters will end badly)
- Sing and dance (music must be silent)
- Wear costumes (fun fashion forbidden)
- Do not attract the attention of the VOIDS!

Published by the Mayor of Igloo City

Riya rolled her eyes. 'Wow, this place sounds like a hoot,' she said.

Will cast his mind back to their frightening clashes with the Voids in the Whispering Wood and the Fire Desert. 'I don't know, sounds sensible to me,' he retorted. 'If it protects everyone from those robot spiders.'

A few minutes later, Sam came to a slippery stop and peered into the semi-darkness over the igloos. 'There's something up ahead,' he whispered. 'Lots of black blobs, standing like soldiers on parade.'

Will clenched his jaw. It didn't sound like Voids, so what new enemy was this? 'Sam, get your head down and let's take a closer look,' he said.

They weaved between a few more igloos and suddenly found themselves in a huge town square. Will sighed with relief. The animals hadn't run away. They were all here! There were hundreds of penguins, all standing in neat rows and staring up at a raised ice platform. At the end of each row of penguins stood a polar wolf wearing a metal helmet

with a blade like a short mohican. The wolves were watching the penguins with their piercing yellow eyes.

'This is weird. What are they all doing?' asked Riya suspiciously.

'I'm not sure about this, Will,' Sam said. 'My ossicones are still jingle-jangling.'

'Yeah, maybe we shouldn't just go barging in,' added Riya.

Will gave her a look of disbelief. 'I never thought I'd hear *you* say that,' he said. 'Come on, you two. We've found everyone, and I promised to help, that's what matters. Let's find out who's in charge.' He strode forwards. 'Hey, hi everyone!'

As they reached the first row of penguins, a ripple of noise passed through the crowd. Some of the penguins squawked and flapped their little wings excitedly. Their whispers grew louder and louder.

'It's him!' exclaimed one. 'The Night Zookeeper.'

'Look at his beautiful coat,' said another.

The penguins broke ranks and began to close in on him. Will was surprised that some of them were nearly as tall as he was. He heard one of the polar wolves howl and others were barking and growling.

'The badge on his cap is so shiny,' said another voice. The penguins were jostling Will now. 'We'd never be allowed a cap like that!'

Will was beginning to feel trapped as black-and-white bodies bumped into each other and him. 'Hey, wait a minute,' he protested. He glanced over his shoulder to see that Riya and Sam were also both being mobbed by the excited penguins. 'Hey, back off, Waddles!' he heard Riya say.

Suddenly, Will felt something grab his collar. He tried to twist away, but there was a rush of air and he was lifted off his feet. 'Thanks, Sam,' he called out, thinking the young giraffe had come to his rescue again. But as he rose higher, to his surprise, he swung round and spotted Sam still in the crowd of penguins. There was a beating of powerful wings above him and Will felt his feet touch down on top of the ice platform. Now the penguins were pointing up at him, all shouting and squawking loudly. The helmeted wolves were snapping at them, trying to restore some order. Will turned to see who had carried him up through the air. Next to him, there was a large, white owl wearing a beautiful, silver breastplate. She raised one wing tip into the cold air. Immediately, the crowd fell silent and the penguins shuffled hurriedly back into line. Will couldn't help being impressed. She reminded him of one of his teachers, Mrs Barnes, who could silence a school assembly with a single stare. This owl was definitely in charge. A little nervously, Will stretched out a hand. 'How do you do?' he said, as politely as he could.

The owl turned her neck to look at him with round, orange eyes. Her stare was neither friendly nor unfriendly, but it was so intense that Will dropped his gaze. Then she blinked and smiled. 'Welcome, Night Zookeeper,' she said. 'My name is Circles. I am the Mayor of Igloo City. It's a pleasure to meet you.' She held out her wing and Will shook it enthusiastically.

'You too,' he said.

Circles turned to face the crowd below. 'Citizens of Igloo City!' she boomed. 'This is indeed a joyful night. Help has arrived in our darkest hour. Friends, I present to you . . . our

Night Zookeeper!' Circles flung out a wing towards Will. The huge crowd of penguins cheered and clapped their flippers together as one. Even the wolves threw back their heads and howled their approval. Will felt his cheeks burning with so many eyes on him. 'Oh, happy times!' cried Circles. 'At last, the gates shall soon be opened!' The crowd cheered even louder and in places the penguins began to sing and dance.

A flash of anger passed across Circles' face. Her chest heaved under her armoured breastplate as she took a deep breath and bellowed, 'Stop! Have you forgotten our rules so quickly? We're not safe yet.' Again, the crowd fell instantly still and silent. 'Remember: you must not attract attention!' the owl berated the audience. 'No singing! No dancing! These rules are for your own good! Now return to your homes, citizens.' Will watched as the penguins began to shuffle off into the lanes, muttering and whispering.

'Come, Night Zookeeper,' said Circles, staring directly at him again. 'We have much to discuss.'

Chapter Two

Circles led Will towards the rear of the platform. Ahead of them was a bridge leading to a huge building. It was much grander than the surrounding igloos, with tall columns and owl figures carved into the facade.

'I'm so glad you're here,' said Circles.

Will was still looking up at the impressive

building. 'Is that your house?' he asked. 'It's amazing.'

Circles nodded. 'Thank you. I never asked for any of this, you know,' she said with a sigh. 'But the citizens of Igloo City insisted and built it for me as a reward.'

'Really? What for?' Will asked.

'My victory,' she replied and tapped a wing tip against her silver breastplate.

Will examined the piece of armour more closely. His eyes widened. 'Is that what I think it is?' he asked in amazement. 'Is that Nulth metal?'

'From a Void,' Circles confirmed proudly.

'I defeated one in battle and made this armour from a piece of it. The penguins repaid me for my bravery by putting me in charge.'

Will's mouth hung open in astonishment. 'That's incredible!' he said. This Circles was obviously a great ally to have in his fight against Nulth's forces. 'But how did you defeat it?'

'If you don't mind, that's a story for later. We have a pressing problem to solve.' Circles leaned her head close to Will's ear. 'There are enemies within the city walls,' she said in a low voice. 'Rebels have locked the gate and stolen the key. We are all trapped.'

'But some sick animals managed to reach the hospital in the Fire Desert,' said Will. 'How did they manage to escape?'

'It's a mystery,' she replied with a frown. 'I think they sneaked out just before the gates were sealed.'

'You must have been pleased,' said Will.

'Oh, yes,' she said. 'Delighted. But now we must get the key back.'

A long snout with a lolling tongue appeared next to them. Sam had raised his head up to the platform. 'Well, that's why we're here,' he said cheerily. 'We've come to help.'

Circles bristled her feathers. 'Take that mask

off at once,' she demanded. 'No costumes are allowed here.'

'What, this?' said Sam, pointing at the dark markings around his eyes. 'It's not a costume. It's because I'm a spying giraffe.'

'A spy!' exclaimed Circles. 'Remove your mask immediately.' She hopped up onto Sam's snout.

Sam went cross-eyed as he tried to focus on the angry owl. 'Hey, get off,' he exclaimed. 'Your talons are tickling my nose!' He spotted Circles' sharp beak. 'Right, that's it, I'm off!' he said. Sam squeezed his eyes shut in concentration.

'I said take the mask off,' growled Circles. 'You must follow the rules too. Hey, what's happening?'

Sam had begun to fade from view. Circles took off in alarm. The outline of Sam's body glowed for a second and then he turned completely invisible. Circles fluttered down next to Will and blinked in confusion at the empty space where Sam had been. Will covered his mouth to hide a smile. Circles turned on Will. 'You brought a spy here?' she snapped. 'What were you thinking?'

Will was taken aback. Again, Circles reminded him of strict Mrs Barnes at school.

He felt a bit scared and a bit in awe at the same time. 'Sorry,' he replied. 'That's just one of Sam's tricks. He's harmless. Really, we're here to help you.'

Suddenly, there was a lot of shouting below.

'What's the problem now?' said Circles irritably. She hopped into the air and flew down towards the commotion.

Will moved to the edge of the platform. He spotted Riya. She was surrounded by three growling polar wolves. 'Stay back! I'm friends with the Night Zookeeper,' she shouted crossly.

'Sam! Are you still there?' Will called out quickly.

'Sure thing,' replied Invisible Sam. Will felt Sam's warm breath on his face.

'Lift me down there, quickly. Riya's causing trouble.'

Will ran across the square towards Riya. The wolves were howling their complaints to Circles.

'She won't do as she's ordered, boss,' one of them said. 'She wouldn't stop.'

'Oi! I don't answer to you,' said Riya defiantly. 'Who put you in charge?'

'She was telling a story, boss,' barked another wolf. 'Stories aren't allowed.'

Will stopped next to Circles. 'Hey, it's okay,

she's with me,' he said.

Circles ignored him. 'Continue your report,' she said to the wolf.

By now, the argument had drawn a large crowd of penguins back out of their igloos.

'The girl was describing a purple elephant to this citizen,' said the wolf. Will looked down and saw a small, fluffy creature cowering next to the wolf. The poor baby penguin looked terrified.

'I haven't done anything wrong,' protested Riya. 'I was telling him about your painting, Will.'

'Painting is banned,' howled the wolf.

'Purple is dangerous,' growled another.

Riya persisted, 'That's all I said, Will, and how elephants are scared of tiny mice!'

There were several cries of shock in the surrounding crowd and all the penguins began to mutter loudly. One of the polar wolves curled back its lips and snarled at Riya, 'Traitor!'

Will watched in shock as another wolf sprang forward and tried to grab Riya's arm with its yellow fangs. Riya dodged out of reach just in time. 'Don't you touch me, you stinking furball,' she shouted. Another cry of

shock echoed through the crowd.

'Enough!' bellowed Circles. The crowd fell silent. Will looked around at the trembling penguins and the furious wolves. He rushed forwards. Even though he was cross with Riya—she was making things worse every time she opened her mouth—he had to calm things down. They were here to help, not cause a fight. He placed himself between Riya and the wolves and faced Circles.

'Circles, I don't know what the problem is,' he said as firmly as he could, 'but Riya is my friend, and if you want my help . . .' Circles stared directly at him for what seemed like ages. Will could feel the tension in the air as the crowd held its breath. 'Tell them to leave her alone, please,' he pleaded.

Several more seconds passed in tense silence. Then Circles gave a curt nod. The wolves immediately turned tail and slunk away. 'And the rest of you,' Circles said to the crowd. 'Go home immediately, citizens.'

The crowd of penguins shuffled off. Will glared at Riya. 'What are you doing?' he said fiercely. 'You're embarrassing me in front of Circles.'

Riya looked at him in shock. 'Embarrassing you?' she spluttered.

Will ignored her and turned to Circles. 'Thank you,' he said. 'I'm sure Riya is sorry for causing a fuss.' He could feel Riya's angry eyes boring into the back of his neck.

'It's quite alright, Night Zookeeper,' replied Circles evenly. 'Riya was not to know.'

'Know what exactly?' said Riya, coming to stand by Will.

'You must understand, young lady, that everything I do, I do for them.' Circles gestured towards the sea of igloos. 'To keep them safe. The rules are for them. And they're for you, Riya. For your own protection, of course.'

'And which of your stupid rules did I break

exactly?' Riya snapped, simmering with fury.

'Riya, please,' hissed Will in exasperation. 'Calm down. Circles is not the enemy.'

Circles leaned towards them and lowered her voice. 'You used a word that should never be used. You spoke of a creature that has brought chaos and disorder to Igloo City. The rebel who has trapped us all inside the City.' Her voice was barely a whisper. 'You mentioned The Mouse!'

Chapter Three

Will and Riya looked at each other in surprise.

'A mouse?' repeated Will.

'Keep your voice down,' warned Circles. 'Not just any mouse. The Mouse.' Riya tried not to giggle. Circles glared at her. 'Follow me,' she ordered. 'Let's go inside where we can talk in private.'

Circles led Will and Riya up a long flight of snowy stairs towards her grand house. Riya tugged at Will's arm to make him fall back a few steps behind Circles.

'Will, I don't like what's going on here,' she said under her breath. 'It's like Sam said. There's something fishy about all this. Where is that clumsy giraffe anyway?'

'He went invisible,' replied Will. 'You don't get it, Riya. Circles is protecting everyone. Her rules keep the Voids away. See?' Will pointed at a nearby poster, which read: *Say Please and Thank You, Do Your Best,* and *Circles Means Safety.*

'Yeah, and what about that one?' retorted Riya. She gestured to another poster with the words: *Always Listen to Circles and Never Ever Question Her Rules!* 'Who does she think she is?'

complained Riya.

'She's a hero,' snapped Will. 'See her armour? It's from a Void. She defeated one in battle. She told me.'

Riya raised her eyebrows. 'And you believed her, right?'

Will was getting really annoyed with Riya now. 'Yes, I do!' he hissed. 'Look around. See any Voids? Any Gunk? Any poisonous water or grey fog? No? So, Circles must be doing something right. Right?'

Riya grunted and looked away.

'Welcome to my headquarters,' announced Circles and they followed her inside the huge building. As they passed along a corridor, Will spotted a number of other posters on the icy walls. One stood out immediately. It read *WANTED* in large capitals and featured a drawing of a vicious-looking creature. It had shifty eyes, tattered ears, uneven whiskers and a pair of fangs like long needles. Its body was muscular, its feet had long, dirty claws and the end of its tail was shaped like a snake's head. There was a height chart behind the animal, like Will had seen in police photos of suspects. He looked at the scale in astonishment. This nasty-looking creature was nearly two metres tall!

WANTED

6.2

6.1

6.0

5.9

Circles had noticed Will examining the poster. "Ahhh, yes," she said. 'There he is. My sworn enemy and yours, the traitor, Eek the Eskimouse!'

'Wow, what's he been eating for breakfast?' remarked Riya.

'Well, there are rumours,' began Circles and stopped herself. 'No, I shouldn't say. It's too unpleasant.'

'It's okay, Circles,' said Will. 'I want to know what we're up against here.'

Circles sighed and lowered her voice again. 'There are rumours that The Mouse feasts upon . . . well, remember your fluffy friend outside?' Will's eyes grew wide. 'Yes, disgusting, I know,' confirmed Circles sadly. 'It's horrible. Savage!'

'Yeah, right,' muttered Riya under her breath. 'A penguin-munching mouse. Sure.'

Circles led them into a large room. A wall of

ice blocks had been polished so much that they were now as clear as glass. They formed a window with wide views across the whole of Igloo City. 'There,' said Circles, pointing a wing tip across the rooftops. In the distance, Will and Riya could see a pair of large gates in the city walls. 'Eek has the key. Until we get it back, we are all trapped in the city, held hostage by that vicious traitor. Who knows what terrible plans he has? Who knows when he will strike next? Night Zookeeper, you must help the terrified citizens of my city. Help me. Help us all. Do your duty, find the key and set us free!'

Riya whispered in Will's ear, 'Do you really believe any of this Eek nonsense?'

Circles turned her head to fix Riya with a cold stare. 'You do know that owls have fantastic hearing, don't you?'

'Oops,' said Riya.

'I've been listening to all of your comments and complaints,' continued Circles, her feathers bristling. 'I must say it is very rude. First, you break the rules and I forgive you. Then you come into my house and you insult me. Who do you think you are, young lady?'

'I'm sorry,' said Will hurriedly. 'We didn't mean to upset you.'

'You need to find Eek and get that key, Night Zookeeper,' said Circles. 'Is that too much to ask?'

'No, no, of course not,' replied Will. 'I promise we'll get it back.'

'Yes, yes, get it back for me,' said Circles enthusiastically.

Riya narrowed her eyes. 'And for all the other animals, right? To help them.'

'Of course, them too,' said Circles. 'Now hurry, before that rebel mouse brings more chaos to this poor city.'

Will and Riya descended the snowy steps to

the town square.

'So, where are we going?' asked Riya. Will didn't reply. 'Will? What's the problem?'

Will turned to her. 'Why are you being like this?' he snapped. 'Causing trouble all the time?'

Riya glared at him. 'Because I don't trust her,' she said in a low, angry voice.

'Well, you're wrong!' he replied. 'You were wrong about Captain Claw. And you're wrong about Circles too. I'm going to help her and the penguins like I promised. I can save them from this Eek.'

Riya crossed her arms. 'Alright, hero,

whatcha gonna do?'

Will reached into his pocket and pulled out the Orb his grandma had given him. 'This,' he replied firmly. He lifted the globe to his forehead and closed his eyes. Bright colours began to swirl inside the glass and Will saw a hazy picture in his mind. Gradually, the image

became clear and he could see a flying saucer hovering above a figure on the ground. A beam of green light shot down from the UFO and the figure was lifted off their feet and pulled up into the spaceship. The image then disintegrated and the colours in the Orb faded to grey. Will blinked and frowned.

'Well?' asked Riya. 'What did you see?'

'I don't get it,' Will replied. 'It was a spaceship with a tractor beam.'

'How does that help then?'

Will's head dropped. 'I . . . I don't know. Let's find Sam. Maybe he can use his spying skills.' He put the Orb away and walked towards the igloos. 'Where do you think he might be?' he asked. Riya didn't answer. When Will looked around, he saw that she hadn't moved. 'Hey, what are you doing? We've got to find that key,' Will called back.

'I'm sorry, I don't think that's the job we're here to do,' she said.

Will clenched his jaw. 'Are you coming or not?' he asked.

'No, I'm staying here,' she replied. 'I'm going to keep an eye on that owl.'

'Fine, suit yourself,' snapped Will, turning on his heel. 'I've got a city to save.' He stalked off into the lanes between the igloos without looking back. As he entered the quiet streets, his anger began to fade. Despite his annoyance, he felt a pang of worry and regret that he was going to have to face this terrifying enemy without his friend by his side.

Chapter
Four

Will trudged through the lanes in search of Sam. There was no one about: the penguins had all retreated inside their igloos. The snow was now falling in thick flakes, Will shivered and pulled his Night Zookeeper's coat around him. He wished his uniform was a little warmer. As he made his way through the snow, he felt a strange

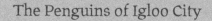

sensation. The jacket began to puff up, as if someone was inflating it from inside. At the same time, he felt warm air begin to circulate around his chest and arms.

'Whoa, I wasn't expecting that,' he said to himself with a smile. 'Built-in central heating. Nice!'

Will stood under one of the orange street lights. There was no sign of Sam. In the silent semi-darkness, Will suddenly felt small and alone. The light above him flickered and faded a little. He wondered about returning to the town square to find Riya. He sighed. Out of the corner of his eye, he spotted a shape in the snow. It was a bit blurred around the edges as the snow was settling, but Will recognized it: a large hoof print. He cast his gaze further and saw another hoof print and another. 'There you are,' Will said, smiling, and set off following Sam's tracks.

A few minutes later, the trail of hoof prints came to a stop. Will bent down and picked up a ball of snow. He aimed at the point where the tracks ended and threw the snowball. It hit an invisible wall and slid to the ground. There was a flash of light and Sam reappeared.

'Found you!' grinned Will. Sam didn't look up. He had bent his neck so low that his huge, flared nostrils were almost touching the snow.

'Hey, what are you doing?' asked Will.

'Spying,' Sam replied. He peered at something on the ground and then took a couple of slow steps forwards.

Will joined him. 'What is it, Sam? I can't see anything. Oh!' Will spotted some tiny, faint tracks in the snow. They looked like a series of dots and dashes.

'Definitely something fishy going on,' muttered Sam as he inspected the marks.

'Something mousy, you mean!' exclaimed Will. 'Well done, Sam. You've found him!'

'I have?' replied Sam in surprise. 'Great. Who?'

'Eek,' said Will. 'Eek!'

Sam gave Will an excited look. 'Ooo, are we doing impressions? I love impressions! Wanna see my impression of a snake?' Sam reared up onto his back legs, tucked his front legs into his sides and made his neck as straight as possible. He then began to wiggle from his hooves to his ossicones. 'Hiss, hiss, I'm a ssssnake!'

Will laughed. 'No, Sam, it wasn't an impression,' he said. 'Eek is an Eskimouse and I reckon these tracks will lead us to him. He's the one who's stolen the key. He's powerful, ugly and six feet tall!'

Sam looked at Will, then looked down at the mouse prints and back to Will. 'He's got tiny feet.'

Will rolled his eyes. 'Those aren't *his* feet, obviously,' he said. 'But they are mouse tracks. We need to follow them before the snow covers them completely. Let's go.'

Will and Sam followed the trail deeper and deeper into the maze of lanes between the igloos.

'Sam, look,' said Will excitedly. 'There's another set of tracks joining this one. We're definitely going the right way.' As they moved on, the tracks became fainter as the snow blanketed the ground. At one point, the trail went dead. Will looked around in frustration, cursing the snow, and then he spotted a single track at the entrance to an alley. 'Quick, up here!' he said. They rushed up the alley and stopped in surprise. It was a dead end. The orange street lights were glowing brighter here than anywhere else in the city. In front of them was a huge wall of thick ice. They had reached the city walls.

Will groaned. 'I don't understand,' he said. 'Where could the mice have gone?'

Sam raised a hoof to his lips and whispered, 'Shhh. Look over there.'

Will and Sam tucked in next to an igloo and watched a tiny shape scurrying along the edge of the city wall. The mouse stopped and stood up on its hind legs, made its paw into a fist and tapped on the ice.

Tap-Tap-Tap-Tap

Tap . . . Tap-Tap . . . Tap

Will and Sam watched in amazement as the ice wall began to glow from within. Strange symbols seemed to float just beneath the surface of the ice: there were pictures of cheese and trumpets and floppy hats and, right in the middle, a huge mug of steaming hot chocolate. The mouse squeaked with excitement, walked straight through the illuminated wall and disappeared. The symbols faded and the ice looked normal again.

'It's like the infinity symbol,' said Will with a grin. 'It's some kind of magic doorway.'

'Mouse Code,' said Sam.

'Sorry?'

'The tapping,' he explained. 'That mouse opened the door by tapping a code. We spies are trained in Mouse Code. Four quick taps, followed by long, short, long, short gaps between taps.'

'Brilliant, Sam!' exclaimed Will.

'It spells the letters H and C,' added the giraffe.

Will's eyes flew open. 'Of course! Hot Chocolate. Like that symbol. Come on, I bet

Eek's inside.' He rushed forwards, held his fist up to the ice and knocked.

Tap-Tap-Tap-Tap

Tap . . . Tap-Tap . . . Tap

Will stepped back and watched with satisfaction as the glowing wall symbols reappeared. 'You ready for this?' he asked Sam grimly. 'Forget Voids. This beast could be our deadliest enemy yet.'

Will walked into the ice wall, except it was no longer solid. He passed straight through the ice into a dark, narrow corridor. He turned round to see Sam's head poking through the icy veil. The giraffe was straining to move forwards.

'I can't . . . urgh . . . I can't fit,' Sam huffed. Will peered through the strange ice lights and frowned. The entrance was far too small for Sam. 'Sorry,' said Sam miserably.

'No, it's not your fault,' replied Will. 'I'd never have found this place without your brilliant spying skills. You never need to be sorry for anything, Sam.'

'But I want to help you fight this Eek monster,' moaned Sam.

'I know, but I've got to do this on my own now,' said Will. 'You go back to the town square and find Riya. Make sure she's not causing any more trouble, okay? I'll see you back there once I've got the key.' He smiled bravely at his friend.

Sam nodded and slowly withdrew his head and neck back through the magic ice door. The lights faded and the corridor became even darker. Will swallowed. He put his hand in his pocket and his fingers closed around his torch. He had to be ready for anything. There was a bright doorway at the far end of the corridor. Will moved cautiously towards it. All of a sudden, a voice echoed off the shadowy walls. Will froze on the spot.

'I have been expecting you, Night Zookeeper,' it said.

Will whipped the torch out of his pocket. 'Come out where I can see you, Eek,' said Will defiantly.

'You followed the tracks as I hoped you would,' came the voice.

Will's legs were shaking. Had he walked into a trap? 'Show yourself!' he cried, his voice cracking.

'I'm right here,' said the voice. Will shielded his eyes as he peered at the bright exit ahead. 'Here!' insisted the voice. 'Oh, for goodness sake. It is dark, isn't it? Hey, guys! Guys! Can someone switch on the corridor lights please? Guys? The lights!' The corridor was suddenly flooded by bright light. 'That's better!' called out the voice cheerfully. Will blinked. The corridor was still empty. 'Yoo-hoo, down here!' said the voice.

Will looked down. There was a small mouse standing a few feet in front of him. Will shook his head. Was he seeing things? He bent down a little to examine the tiny creature more closely. The mouse was dressed in a pair of puffy orange trousers tucked into a pair of luminous snowboots, a multicoloured waistcoat, a long yellow scarf and one of those big bobble hats skiers sometimes wear. He wore a single glittery glove on one paw and had a gold-framed monocle over one eye. He looked as if he'd fallen asleep in a dressing-up box.

'You're . . . you're not Eek,' Will mumbled. The little mouse grabbed the lapels of his waistcoat and yanked it open with a flourish. Underneath was a figure-hugging superhero costume with the gold letters EEK stitched across the chest.

'Ta-daah!' said Eek.

'You . . . you can't be Eek,' spluttered Will. 'Where are your fangs? Your claws?'

'Oh, you've seen that ridiculous poster, haven't you?' said Eek with a grin. 'I particularly like the snake's-head tail Circles gave me. Nice touch. Reeeally scary, huh? Mind you, I wish I had those muscles.' He peered down at his round belly and sighed.

'I don't believe you,' said Will. 'Where's the real Eek?'

Eek rolled his eyes. 'Oh, she's really got to you, hasn't she? Guys. Guys! Come and tell him who I am. But where are my manners? I haven't even offered you a refreshment. Guys, come and welcome our guest.'

Will's eyes widened with alarm. From the doorway, a huge gang of brightly-dressed mice scurried into the corridor. 'Eek, Eek,

Eek!' they all squeaked. They started dancing and singing as they swarmed around Will's feet. Will suddenly felt unsteady, as if he were on soft ground. He looked down and, to his astonishment, he saw that the mice had lifted both of his feet an inch off the floor.

'Whoa, get off,' he said, waving his arms to stop himself toppling over.

'Tallyho!' cried Eek, and the mice began to follow him towards the doorway. Will

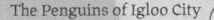

was moving across the floor

as if he were on roller-skates.

'Tallyho! Let's go!' chanted the mice.

Will was transported into a large ice cavern.
It was lit by the same orange street lights but
here they were glowing brightly. Green candles
with purple flames sat on top of rainbow-
coloured icicles. Carved into one wall was a
luminous map of the whole of Igloo City. Eek
presented the room with a sweep of his arm
and said, 'Welcome, Night Zookeeper.
Welcome to the Igloo City Resistance!'

Chapter Five

The horde of mice under Will's feet put him down. 'The Igloo City Resistance?' said Will crossly. 'You're just a bunch of rebels keeping everyone prisoner! Circles warned me about you.'

'I bet she did,' said Eek with a chuckle. He scurried up a tall icicle and flopped back in a tiny armchair. 'Resistance, rebels, it's all the same thing, really,' he said casually. 'We certainly don't listen to Circles and her joy-sucking, life-limiting, fun-ruining rules, do we guys?'

'NO!' the huge crowd of mice cried.

'Then you admit it,' said Will in astonishment. 'Well, you're up against me now. You're up against the Night Zookeeper!'

At that moment, a voice broke into song:

Hot chocolate, hot chocolate
Warms you in the snow
And makes the street lights glow.
Hot chocolate, hot chocolate

Helps you when you're low
And makes your ideas grow.

An old penguin with half-moon spectacles waddled towards Will with a smile. 'You're here at last,' he said. 'Wonderful! They call me the Professor. This is for you.' He held out a mug towards Will. The aroma of hot chocolate wafted into Will's nostrils. It smelt rich and comforting and Will's mouth watered immediately.

Will shook his head. 'Is this a trick?' he said. 'I've

come for the key. Now where is it?'

'Wow, you really need to relax, kid,' drawled Eek. 'Chill out and enjoy yourself.'

'Go on,' said the penguin gently. 'Have some. It's one of my special potions, isn't it, Eek?'

Eek grinned. 'The best,' he said.

'Makes your tongue tingle!' shouted one of the other mice.

'And your teeth grin!' cried another.

'And your stomach sing!'

'And your brain buzz with bubbles!'

This time, everyone began to sing:

Hot chocolate, hot chocolate

How we love you so

Cos you make the good times flow!

'Take a sip, kid,' said Eek. 'You know you want to.'

'Stop calling me kid,' snapped Will. 'I'm the Night Zookeeper! You can't keep me prisoner here.'

Eek shrugged. 'Who's keeping you prisoner? You can leave now if you want. You know where the door is.'

Will looked about suspiciously. The mice were chatting and laughing amongst themselves. For a bunch of vicious rebels, they all seemed rather . . . friendly. For the first time, a feeling of doubt seeped into his mind.

The Professor gave him a kind smile and held out the mug towards him. 'It's getting cold,' he said softly. The rich, chocolatey smell was intoxicating and Will couldn't resist any longer. He reached out slowly and took it. He raised the steaming mug to his lips and took a sip. It was velvety

smooth and utterly delicious. He took a larger gulp. The luxurious chocolate flavour danced across his tongue and the hot, creamy milk washed down his throat like a glorious wave. He drank some more and gasped with surprise. The mice hadn't been exaggerating: his tongue was tingling, his tummy felt warm and satisfied and his spirits soared. He broke out in a grin. 'Wow,' he whispered. 'That's the best hot chocolate I've ever tasted.'

'Told you,' said Eek. 'The best!'

The Professor nodded with satisfaction. 'I'm glad you like it, Night Zookeeper,' he said. 'It helps us keep our spirits up when we're stuck in here hiding from that owl.'

As Will drank some more, he spotted something out of the corner of one eye. Hanging high up on a wall, there was a large iron key on a hook. Will suddenly remembered where he was. And why he had come. He threw the mug of hot chocolate down on the floor. A group of mice squealed and scattered out of the way. 'Oh, I get it,' he said furiously. 'How could I have been so stupid? This *is* a trick, isn't it? Giving me hot chocolate, getting me to relax, pretending

83

to be friendly. And all this time, you're keeping everyone prisoner in this city. Circles was right. You did steal it. I can see it over there. You do have the key!'

Eek glanced over his shoulder at the hanging key. 'Did I ever say we didn't?' said the mouse.

'How dare you lock everyone up?' Will challenged.

'It's for their own protection,' replied Eek. 'Besides, we're all prisoners while Circles is in charge.'

Will glared at the tiny mouse. 'No, Circles' rules are to protect everyone and you keep breaking them.'

'What, like your friend, you mean?' retorted Eek. 'Seems like she doesn't play by the rules. That can land you in a whole world of trouble around here.'

A fizz of fear swept away Will's anger in an instant. 'Riya,' he said under his breath. 'What do you mean?'

The Professor sighed. He took off his half-moon glasses and cleaned them. 'It wasn't wise to leave her on her own,' he said. 'You don't make trouble for Circles and get away with it.'

'Too right,' said Eek. 'You're wasting your time with this key business. You should be more worried about your friend.'

Will shook his head. 'No, no, you're both trying to trick me. Nice try, but I'm going to take that key and you can't stop me.'

'That really isn't a good idea,' said Eek.

Will strode towards the wall. He immediately realized that the key was far too high up for him to reach. He clenched his jaw. The Professor bustled up beside him. 'Night Zookeeper, you mustn't take the key,' he urged. 'We're not the enemy. It's Circles.'

'I don't believe you,' said Will. 'She's

not the one locking everyone up.' He searched for a solution to reaching the key. How was he going to get it down?

'You mustn't trust that owl,' said the penguin professor.

'She defeated a Void in battle,' snapped Will. 'Is that who you're all working for? Nulth and the Voids?'

The penguin shook his head and spoke slowly and deliberately. 'You know, no one ever witnessed it. This battle of hers.'

'What?' said Will. He was concentrating so hard on thinking of a way to lift the key down that he was hardly listening any more.

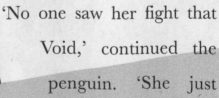

'No one saw her fight that Void,' continued the penguin. 'She just

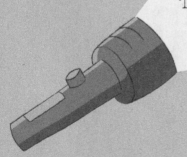

appeared one night wearing that armour and took over.'

Will's mind suddenly flashed back to his vision in the Orb: the beam of light from the UFO lifting the figure into the air. He smiled to himself. Now he understood. This was what he was meant to do. He'd seen it in the Orb. Will pulled his torch out of his pocket. He pressed the button down and a beam of brilliant light shot across the room. 'Ooooooh!' said the mice in unison. Will aimed the beam at the key. It glistened in the light. Imagining the beam was like the light from the UFO, Will concentrated on the thought of lifting the key off the hook. The light turned from white to green and the key began to rattle. Slowly the key rose up so that it was no longer dangling from the hook. Will pictured it levitating from the wall towards him and it responded. It was as if he were controlling it with his imagination. The key floated along the path of the green beam and straight into Will's outstretched hand. 'Uh-oh!' said the mice.

'Gotcha!' said Will triumphantly. He immediately broke into a sprint towards the magic ice-door. Behind him, the mice squeaked in alarm. He heard the Professor call out, 'Stop, please, you don't know what you're doing.'

Will ignored them. It was time to find his friends, return the key and free Igloo City.

Chapter Six

Will rushed back towards the town square. There was still no one about. He wanted to find Riya and Sam to tell them how he hadn't fallen for Eek's trickery. He had the key and now he could help Circles set the penguins free. He picked up his pace in his excitement.

As he reached the end of a lane, he heard a

low murmuring ahead. Will entered the town square and skidded to a halt. The penguins had all gathered around the raised platform again. Some of them glanced back at him but quickly looked away again. They wouldn't meet his gaze. Will looked up at the platform and gasped in shock. Fear trickled down his spine like ice-cold water. A metal crane had been wheeled out to the edge of the platform. Circles was standing in front of it, puffing out her armoured chest. Swinging slowly from the arm of the crane was a large rope net. And inside the net were Riya and Sam.

Will's heart hammered inside his ribcage.

He tried to shout but his voice was strangled in his throat. He could see Circles smirking at him. He stumbled forwards through the penguins, who stood aside with their heads bowed. He could hear Sam and Riya's muffled protests. The net swung as Sam shifted his position and Riya stared fearfully at the drop below the net.

Will gulped and finally managed to shout, 'What are you doing? Let my friends go!'

Circles laughed. 'You might want to choose your words more carefully, boy,' she sneered. 'Take a look. My polar wolves have been busy.'

The crowd of penguins parted silently in front of Will to reveal the spot directly below the net. Several polar wolves were gathered around a large pool of dark blue water. One of the wolves was stabbing the sharp blades of its helmet over and over into the ground. Chunks of ice were splintering away as it worked to make the ice-cold pool larger. The wolf raised its head and stared at Will. It pulled back its top lip in a sinister smile.

'Circles, I don't understand. What's happening here?' cried Will.

'Easy. This is what happens to spies,' she replied.

'Please, Circles, there must be a mistake,' pleaded Will. 'We're all on your side. Look, I've got the key.' Will held the key high above his head. A murmur of excitement rushed through the crowd. The polar wolves yapped and howled and Circles flew up into the air. 'Here,' Will called up to her. 'You can free the city now!' Will shot a glance at Sam and Riya. To his surprise, both of them were shaking their heads and desperately trying to shout something.

'Citizens!' boomed Circles. The penguins

and wolves fell silent and stared up at her. She was hovering above the crane, her eyes shining. 'Tonight is the night you have been waiting for! The night when I will finally restore order after the chaos. The defeat of the vicious rebels is at hand. Tonight, we open the gates. Night Zookeeper, give me that key!'

Will was still looking at his friends. They were shaking their heads even more and pleading with their eyes. It was clear what they meant: do not hand over the key to Circles. Will blinked in confusion. He had been so sure. Circles was just protecting people with her rules, wasn't she? Eek had locked everyone up, hadn't he? Eek's words came back to him: *it's for their own protection.* Protection? Protection from what, he wondered.

'Hand me the key, boy!' screeched Circles high above.

Will looked up at the hovering owl. Orange light glinted off her armoured breastplate. The Professor's words echoed in his mind. Words that he had barely heard at the time: *no one ever saw her fight that Void.* Will's heart sunk to his boots. If Circles hadn't defeated a Void, then what was she doing wearing Nulth metal? Will slowly lowered the key and clutched it to his chest.

'No,' he said, his voice tight in his throat.

Circles glared down at him. 'What?'

'No,' he repeated more firmly. 'Where did you get that armour, Circles?'

Circles swooped down in front of him. 'I don't have time for this, boy. Give me the key.'

'You never fought a Void, did you?' accused Will. The crowd groaned with shock. 'You lied to everyone, didn't you? So, if you didn't win the armour in battle, someone must have given it to you.'

'Stop right there,' said Circles. 'I thought it might come to this.' She flew up and perched on the crane arm above the net and the freezing pool. 'There is a bolt—a single bolt—holding this net in place,' she called out menacingly. 'Give me the key or I really will let your friends go!' Riya and Sam twisted and struggled inside the net, sending it spinning and swinging wildly. 'The key, now, or your friends become ice cubes,' said Circles, who bent forwards and grasped the end of the bolt in her sharp beak.

'No!' cried Will in horror. 'Stop! Stop! You win! Here, here, it's yours. Take it.'

'No, Will, don't do it,' cried Riya breathlessly.

'Be quiet, girl,' snapped Circles. 'Last chance, Night Zookeeper.'

'I don't have a choice,' Will called up to Riya. He held the key up in front of him. Circles' eyes flashed, she spread her wings and dived towards him.

'No, Will!' said Riya. 'Eek wasn't locking everyone in. He was locking something out!'

Before Will could react, the key was wrenched from his grasp. Circles spiralled back up into the air, laughing, with the key firmly in her talons. 'Now, my dear citizens, none of you will ever dare break my rules again! Prepare to bow down to the forces of Nulth!' she cried and swooped towards the gates to open them.

Will stood frozen on the spot. How had he got it all so wrong? Why hadn't he listened to Riya's suspicions and the Professor's pleas? He hadn't set the city free: he had delivered it into the hands of his worst enemy! Will stared in horror at the scene unfolding in the square. At the mention of Nulth's name, the penguins had burst into a panic. They waddled and flapped in all directions, screeching and squawking. The wolves rushed away from the pool to chase and harry the penguins for fun. A tall penguin banged into Will in its desperation to reach its igloo, knocking him sideways. He had to do something. He broke into a run to follow Circles towards the gate.

'Wait, Will!' Riya called out. 'Where are you going?'

'I've . . . I've got to stop her,' he stammered.

'Now you're making me even more mad,' Riya shouted. 'Stop trying to do everything on your own, will you? Get us down!'

Will nodded. She was right. He had been too busy being the hero. Too busy acting as if he knew best because he was the Night

Zookeeper. He remembered something his grandma had once told him: *we don't learn from talking; we learn from listening.* He should have listened to his friend and he needed her help more than ever now.

Will rushed towards the pool, weaving between the panicking penguins, and pulled out the torch. 'If it worked for the key . . .' he said to himself and switched on the torch. The super-bright beam shot out and Will aimed it up at the net. He recalled the vision of the UFO again. The beam turned from white to luminous green and lit up the entire net. The torch shook violently in Will's grasp.

This was much harder than lifting the key down. Just imagine it, Will told himself. *All you need to do is believe.* The bolt holding the net in place suddenly pinged away. The net dropped towards the ice pool as Will struggled to

control the huge, heavy object. 'Whoa!' cried
Riya. Will closed his eyes, slowed his breathing
and focused on his imagination. The net
floated gently down, guided by the green torch
beam, until it touched down on solid ice next
to the pool.

Will turned off the torch, and rushed towards his friends. 'About time,' she said crossly. 'I've got bruises all over from clumsy long-legs here.' She dug an elbow into Sam's ribs.

'Thank you, Will, thank you,' he beamed. He shot out his long, wet tongue.

'Oh no, no, no,' said Will, squirming out

of the way just in time and Sam ended up licking Riya's cheek and ear instead.

Riya glared at him furiously. 'That's it, Lankenstein! I'll get you for that.'

'Oh no,' said Will again.

Chapter
Seven

Will was facing the row of igloos at the edge of the square. Thick, grey fog was rolling in dark clouds from the lanes and over the rooftops. The penguins in the square had stopped moving. They watched nervously as the fog tumbled across the ice. Even the polar wolves looked wary. There were noises coming from amongst the sea of igloos: clanking and hissing, the sound of metal scraping on ice and another noise that Will recognized immediately.

Clicker-clacker!   Clicker-clacker!

The fog sitting above the rooftops stretched back all the way to the city walls. A host of crimson lights lit up the fog from within until it glowed blood-red. Will gasped at the size of the approaching army of Voids. He had never seen them in such numbers.

Suddenly, dozens of squawking penguins burst out of the fog back into the square. And then came the giant robot spiders: the Voids scuttled out of the lanes, their red eyes burning with the excitement of the chase. Some of them leapt into the air over the petrified penguins, trailing webs of glistening cables behind them. There was utter confusion and panic as the penguins tried to escape.

Will heard a voice below him. He looked down to see a group of brightly dressed mice at his feet. In the centre of the group was Eek in a bright pink puffer jacket. For once, the mouse looked a bit tense.

'See what you did?' Eek said.

'Yeah, hate to say I told you so,' muttered Riya.

'I'm sorry, both of you,' said Will miserably. 'What have I done?'

'Forget what you've done,' said Eek. 'It's what you do now that's important. Where's that torch of yours?'

'I can't do this on my own,' said Will, shaking his head. He turned to Eek and Riya and Sam. 'I will always need your help.'

'You've got it,' said Sam. 'Team Night Zoo reporting for duty!'

'Okay,' said Will. 'Eek, can you try to get

some of the penguins to safety in your headquarters?'

Eek gave a flamboyant salute, issued some orders to the other mice and they scurried off into the fray.

'Riya, can you distract the Voids somehow? I think if I can get to Circles, it might stop all this.'

Riya nodded. 'Hmm, I've got an idea,' she replied. 'All I need is a pair of ice skates.' She sprinted forwards, looked to her left and then to her right and stopped. She raised her fingers to the corners of her mouth and whistled loudly. Two polar wolves on opposite sides of her raised their helmeted heads. They glared at her with their fierce yellow eyes. 'Yeah, that's it, you two overgrown, tin-brained chihuahuas!' she shouted at them. 'Come and get me!' Enraged, the polar wolves charged towards her at full pelt from both sides. Riya stood her ground, calmly checking from side to side. The wolves covered the ground at remarkable speed, getting closer and closer until they both leapt up at Riya's throat. At exactly the same moment, Riya threw herself to the floor. The polar wolves smacked heads with a clang like a church bell above Riya.

They both tumbled onto the ice, knocked out cold. Riya reached out to remove their bladed helmets. 'Thank you!' she said brightly and quickly stuck her feet inside the upturned helmets. 'Wish me luck,' she called over her shoulder to Will and Sam and skated off towards the Voids. Riya swept across the ice elegantly, vaulted over a penguin and sent a shower of ice spraying up at the nearest Void. The Void instantly swiped at her but she ducked under its metal belly. The robot hissed with anger and spun round just as Riya slalomed back through its legs. The Void twisted and swiped and ended up collapsing in a heap. Will and Sam watched in amazement as Riya continued to duck and swerve and twirl and leap amongst the confused Voids, who went crashing into walls and falling over each other as they tried to chase her.

'Wow, I guess those Saturday skating lessons are working out,' said Will.

'Go Riya!' shouted Sam in encouragement.

Will suddenly heard a voice high above. 'That's it!' Circles cried, hooting with delight. 'Capture the penguins! Round up those mice! Search the city from top to bottom and grab that irritating girl! My deal with Nulth is complete. Soon no penguin, mouse or child will ever question my almighty rule!'

'Okay, now's our chance, Sam,' said Will. 'Let's give that owl a scowl!'

'But she's too high,' said Sam. 'Even I can't reach her.'

Will gripped his torch. 'Well, if it worked for the key and it worked for you . . .' he said. 'Just be ready when I say, okay?'

Will filled his mind with the UFO vision once more and aimed the torch directly at the gloating owl. He pressed the button. Circles was immediately caught in the brilliant beam. 'No!' she cried, dazzled by the light. For a second, she fluttered around in confusion, before recovering and beating her wings powerfully to get clear of the beam.

'No, you don't,' said Will under his breath and adjusted his aim to keep Circles firmly in the light. The torch beam shifted from white to green. Circles squawked and hooted in desperation, fighting to escape like a fish on a line. The torch buzzed and bucked in Will's hand. Try as he might, she was strong and he couldn't pull her down from the air. Will focused on making the torch beam as powerful as the tractor beam of the UFO. Slowly, inch by inch, he began to reel Circles in closer to the ground.

'No, no!' she cried.

Will's hand was burning with the effort, but he kept the torch button pressed down. Circles was pulled lower and lower. Just a few more feet, Will thought. 'Now!' he shouted. Beside him, standing on the tips of his hooves, Sam reached out and grabbed Circles' tail feathers with his teeth.

'Get off me, you slobbery, spaghetti-legged traitor!' screeched Circles, lashing out with her talons.

Sam swung his head and neck sideways, flinging Circles into the wall of an igloo. She crashed into it beak-first with her wings and feet outstretched. For a second, she remained there, flattened against the ice, and then she started to slide down the wall. Her beak and talons ripped through one of her posters as she fell to the floor. Finally, she toppled onto her back and her armoured breastplate broke off and slid away.

'She's out cold,' said Will.

'Team Night Zoo!' replied Sam with a grin. Will raised his hand for a high five. Sam licked it.

'Team Night Zoo,' agreed Will, wiping the sticky saliva on his trousers.

Will's eyes were drawn to something colourful underneath the tattered poster. It was an older poster that had been covered over. Will read the words:

Residents of Igloo City love:

- Painting (the bolder and brighter the better)
- Stories (Happy Ever After and everything in between)
- Dancing (singing and music bring us together)
- Costumes (wear whatever whenever)

Keep the street lights of Igloo City shining bright!

By kind request of The Professor

'Will,' said Sam, biting his bottom lip. 'The Voids. I thought if we stopped Circles, the Voids would stop. They're still attacking.'

Will reread the words at the bottom of the Professor's poster: Keep the street lights shining bright!

'Light,' he said to himself. 'Of course, more light! Sam, come on, we need to find the Professor.'

Chapter Eight

'Over there,' said Will to Sam, pointing. 'We've got to get to the Professor.'

The town square was a scene of chaos and panic. Riya was still distracting some of the Voids, but there were so many of them now, firing out metal webs and leaving trails of grey gunk in the snow. Some of the penguins were trapped in metal cages, whilst Eek was trying to lead the others into the lanes and to the safety of his hidden headquarters.

Will and Sam weaved through the battlefield. Freed from Circles' control, the polar wolves had removed their helmets and joined forces with the penguins and the mice against the army of Voids. 'Professor!' Will shouted. A Void swiped at him and he knocked it aside with a quick blast from his torch. He dashed past and aimed for the Professor, who was surrounded by a group of other eccentrically dressed penguins. It looked as if they were off to a fancy dress party, not a battle: there was a cowboy, a police officer, an army private, a construction worker, a biker in leathers, an astronaut, a footballer, and many more!

Will skidded to a halt in front of them. 'Professor, I need your help.'

'Anything, Night Zookeeper,' replied the Professor. 'What can we do?'

'I saw your poster,' explained Will. 'It's the singing, dancing, painting—all of it—that gives the city its power, isn't it? And that's what powers the street lights, right?'

'Yes, yes, quite right,' said the Professor.

'I've battled Voids before,' said Will. 'They can't stand the light. We can beat them if we can get all the street lights shining as bright as possible. Can you sing your hot chocolate song?'

The Professor clapped his flippers with glee. 'Of course,' he said and turned to the group. 'Everyone, we must sing our song!'

Hot chocolate, hot chocolate
Warms you in the snow
And makes the streetlights glow.

Will looked around. The nearest orange street lights surged and then faded again. 'Louder,' The Professor urged the group. 'Drink your chocolate and raise your voices!'

Again, the nearest street lights shone more strongly, but the others didn't. 'It's no good, Night Zookeeper,' he said, shaking his head. 'We're such a small group of singers, we can't do it on our own. Everyone needs some hot chocolate and everyone needs to sing for this to work.'

An idea leapt into Will's imagination. 'Professor, can you put your mug down on the ice, please, quickly?' he said excitedly. 'I've got an idea.'

The Professor lowered his mug of hot chocolate to the ground. Will pointed his torch down at the mug and pressed the button. Just imagine, he told himself. *All you need to do is believe.* In his mind's eye, Will pictured the mug getting bigger. He imagined it growing and growing and filling to the brim. He could almost smell the amazing aroma. The watching penguins gasped and flapped their wings excitedly. In the torch beam, the mug began to grow. It became wider and taller and fuller and rounder until it was the size of a jacuzzi full of delicious, bubbling, steaming hot chocolate. Will could hardly believe his eyes himself. It had worked perfectly.

'Oooooo!' said the penguins in astonishment.

'Quick, Sam,' said Will. 'We need to bring

all the other penguins over here for a drink. Professor, keep singing and make those street lights glow!'

The penguins took a deep breath and tried to raise their voices above the noise of the battle. The orange street lights nearby began to burn brightly.

Hot chocolate, hot chocolate
Warms you in the snow
And makes the street lights glow.

Guided by Will and Sam, more penguins came to the giant mug and took great, warming mouthfuls of hot chocolate. They huddled together with the others, their spirits lifted, and joined in with the song.

Hot chocolate, hot chocolate
When you're feeling low,
Singing makes our city glow!

'It's working, Professor!' cried Will. 'Look at the lights! Keep singing!'

The fog above the city was glowing again, but this time it was bright orange as the flickering street lights in every lane and alley glowed brighter and brighter. The Voids in the town square had stopped chasing the remaining penguins. They were now scuttling about uncertainly.

'Sing! Sing for your city!' cried the Professor, and the penguins sang prouder and louder still. Will saw Eek and his mice scurry up the sides of the mug and dip their whiskers greedily in the hot chocolate. The mice spread out around the rim of the mug and joined the chorus of happy voices. Some of the polar wolves lapped at the magical liquid, howling in delight at the taste.

Suddenly, every street light in the city burst into brilliant, multicoloured light. Even Will had to shield his eyes. The agitated Voids were stunned by the incredible light show. Their metal bodies buckled and smoked. Their metal webs snapped and crumbled, and the captured penguins waddled out to freedom.

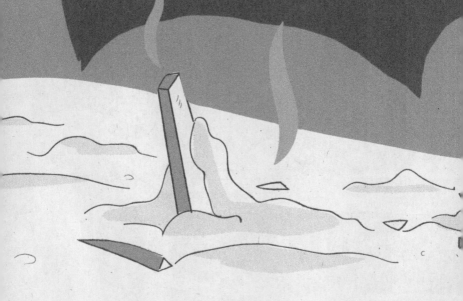

The battle was nearly over: the Voids could not bear the light any longer and they began to run away into the lanes back towards the gate. The fog began to retreat with them.

'We need to follow them!' said Will. 'Push them out of the city.'

'Keep singing!' cried the Professor.

'And dance!' added Eek.

'After them!' shouted Will.

All the animals followed Will and Sam as they charged across the square and between the igloos, singing the hot chocolate song at the tops of their voices. Riya skated up beside them. She was wearing a pirate's hat made from one of Circles' posters.

'Well, everyone else is dressing up, so why not?' she said with a grin.

The residents of Igloo City poured through lanes, all singing and dancing in the bright, colourful light, like an unstoppable carnival. Ahead of the joyful crowd, the Voids were in full retreat, desperate to escape. They poured out through the city gates and onto the icy plains beyond. They slipped and skittered across the ice towards the shrinking fog.

Will slammed the gates shut and everyone cheered.

'Well, they'll think twice about trying to take our city again,' said the Professor happily.

Will turned the key in the lock and turned to him. 'Here,' he said, holding out the key. 'I was wrong about you and Eek. You know best

how to keep Igloo City safe.' Everyone cheered again.

'Thank you, Night Zookeeper,' replied the Professor. 'But it was your idea that saved us. We will always remember that.'

The crowd burst into song again: 'For he's a jolly good fellow, For he's a—'

'Wait!' interrupted Sam. 'Not *for he's.* Freeze! Freeze a jolly good fellow. Geddit? It's so cold here. Freeze a jolly good fellow! Ha ha!'

Riya pulled her paper hat down over her eyes with a groan.

A few minutes later, Will and the others were

back in the square, peering down at Circles, who was waking up.

'Oww, my head!' she mumbled. Without her armour on, she seemed smaller and more fragile. 'What . . . what happened?' she asked meekly.

'I splatted you into a wall,' said Sam.

Circles moaned. 'Why? What did I do? I can't remember anything.'

'How convenient!' said Riya suspiciously.

Will prodded Circles. 'Hey, wake up. You said you did a deal with Nulth. Who is he? What did he want with Igloo City?'

Circles sat up slowly. 'I . . . I . . .' she

stammered. She looked around in shock at the piles of broken Nulth metal and the cheerful, dancing penguins.

'That's right: Igloo City is free again,' said Eek.

'No!' cried Circles. 'Nulth promised me order. All I wanted was control. The Voids were supposed to help me . . .' Her voice trailed off. She glared at them all furiously. 'My armour!' she snapped. 'Give me back my armour! They'll come back, you know. You think some lousy singing and a few silly costumes will scare the Voids off for good? They will be back! He'll send entire legions!' Circles scrambled to her feet and hopped over to her armoured breastplate. She strapped it on and launched herself into the sky. 'You'll be sorry! You'll all be sorry! You need me!' she said, circling over the square.

'Not while we have the Night Zookeeper!' said Sam defiantly.

'I should stop her,' said Will, lifting up his torch.

'No,' said the Professor, lowering Will's torch with his wing. 'She is under the thrall of Nulth. One day, she will see: the only way to drive away the dark is to fill it with light. Forget her for now. It's time to party!' He and Eek went to join all the other dancing, singing residents of Igloo City. Circles beat her wings powerfully and climbed into the sky. Will watched until she was a dot, and then disappeared from view. He frowned.

'What's up?' asked Riya.

'I think that was a mistake,' he said. 'Letting her go. Another mistake. I'm sorry, Riya. I'm really sorry for not believing you. I should've listened.'

'Forget it,' she replied, giving him a friendly slap on the back. 'You made up for it. What I want to know is how you came up with the idea of that massive mug of chocolate. Did you get it from the Orb?'

'No, it wasn't the Orb this time,' Will answered. He thought for a moment. 'D'you know, I don't know where the idea came from. It just popped up in my imagination. With the help of the torch, it worked. No Orb. Just me.'

'Does this mean your powers are getting stronger?' asked Sam.

'I guess so, maybe,' replied Will. Something Grandma Rivers had told him now and then came to mind: *Don't worry about making mistakes, Will. Mistakes have the power to make you better than you were before.*

All of a sudden, the sky blazed with the glowing image of the purple elephant Will had painted.

'It's Maji!' cried Sam.

The purple elephant looked down at them and smiled. Everyone stopped singing and

dancing and looked up in awe. Her voice
boomed across the town square. 'Night
Zookeeper. Please hurry to the Tusk Temple. I
will meet you there.' Maji immediately began
to fade from the sky.

'Wait!' Will called out. 'What am I supposed to do there?'

'Believe. Believe in yourself,' came her faint reply and then she was gone.

'The Tusk Temple,' repeated Sam. 'That's where Maji lives. I wonder why she wants us to go there?'

'For a cup of tea?' replied Riya with a smirk.

'Careful or I'll lick you again,' Sam retorted.

Will switched on his torch and drew the glowing infinity symbol in the air. The scene on the far side of the portal became clearer. Will could see a lush garden of tall hedges, colourful flowers and raked sand. In the distance he spotted a giant purple temple bathed in moonlight. 'Yeah!' said Sam. 'It's Maji's temple! Grass and trees! No more frozen hooves and my ossicones feeling like ice cream cones! Hooray! No offense Professor, Eek.'

'None taken, young man,' replied the penguin professor, contentedly sipping his hot chocolate.

Will looked at the garden scene ahead and the spectacular temple beyond it. 'Ready for another adventure, you two?'

'Team Night Zoo!' Riya and Sam replied in perfect unison. 'Let's do this!'

149

About the Author

By night, Joshua Davidson is the head Night Zookeeper. He works in the Night Zoo and cares for many magical animals such as purple octocows and banana hedgehogs. During his nightly rounds he enjoys playing memory games with the time-travelling elephant and hide and seek with the spying giraffes. Sadly he is yet to win a single game in either contest.

By day, he is an author, artist, game designer and tech entrepreneur. He came up with the idea for nightzookeeper. com, a website where anyone can draw animals and write stories about them, whilst studying an MA in Digital Art at Norwich University of the Arts.

Josh introduced the Night Zoo to Paul, Buzz, Phil and Sam and together they built the Night Zookeeper website, which has since been nominated for a BAFTA, won a London Book Fair award and is currently used in thousands of schools across the world to inspire amazing creative writing.

About the Illustrator

Buzz studied graphic design in Norwich, England where he met Night Zookeeper Josh. Many years later, Josh brought Buzz to the gates of the Night Zoo. Ever since then he has been the regular painter and decorator in the zoo. He draws on his gigantic imagination to care for the animals there and to explore new, previously uncharted parts of the world!

By day, Buzz Burman is a designer and illustrator with a love of clever ideas. As well as drawing what the animals look like in this book, he also designed the cover, the Night Zookeeper website and Night Zookeeper logo!

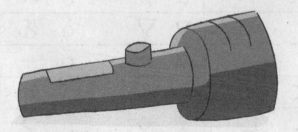

Sam's Code

After discovering Eek's mousecode Sam
created his own secret code.

A	![symbol]	N	![symbol]	1	![symbol]	
B	![symbol]	O	![symbol]	2	![symbol]	
C	![symbol]	P	![symbol]	3	![symbol]	
D	![symbol]	Q	![symbol]	4	![symbol]	
E	![symbol]	R	![symbol]	5	![symbol]	
F	![symbol]	S	![symbol]	6	![symbol]	
G	![symbol]	T	![symbol]	7	![symbol]	
H	![symbol]	U	![symbol]	8	![symbol]	
I	![symbol]	V	![symbol]	9	![symbol]	
J	![symbol]	W	![symbol]	0	![symbol]	
K	![symbol]	X	![symbol]	.	![symbol]	
L	![symbol]	Y	![symbol]	,	![symbol]	
M	![symbol]	Z	![symbol]	?	![symbol]	

Sam has decoded one message already.
Can you figure out the second message?

B E L I E V E

Using Sam's code, work out the
punchline to his jokes.

What made the giraffe late?

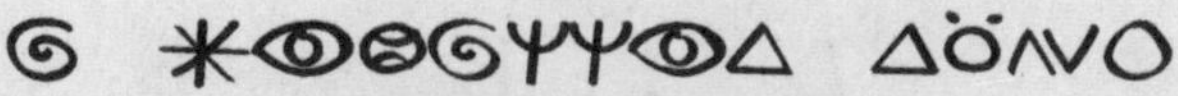

🌀 ✳⊕⊗⊙Ꮆɤɤ⊙△ △ö⋀○

What do you call a royal giraffe?

♀öↂ⊕ ⊗öⱱⒼ▭ ⋀○✳⋔⋀⋀○ꙍ

What's the worst nickname to give a giraffe?

ꙍ▭ⱱ⋔Ɱ⊙⊙⊙♀

Use Sam's code to complete
these challenges:

1. Write your spy name.

2. Write the name of a location
   in the Night Zoo where Sam
   needs to meet you.

3. What do you need to find?

Why not make your own secret code?

Create your own magical animals

At nightzookeeper.com you can test your powers of creativity and invent your own magical zoo animals. Just like yukimura and sparklingfish have done in these stories.

Panda falls in love
By yukimura

Did you know that the panda, who fell in love with the Moon, invented the world's great device, Panwing (which can fly in the sky), before humanity invented their flying machine, the aeroplane? This is the story of the clever panda.

'Moon,' Moss the panda said. He wondered at how big it is, how bright it is, and how powerful it is. Moss fell in love with the Moon.

'Why are you watching the Moon?' his friend asked.
'Because, I . . . I . . . I love the Moon. A . . . actually, I want to marry her,' Moss replied with a shy, small voice.
'What? Do you really want to marry her? Oh, my. But I know you know. You cannot marry her,' the friend told him confidently.

'Why? Why can't I?' Moss really was thinking that he can marry her.

'Because the Moon is sooooooo far from us. If you don't have confidence, just try to touch and sense it. I am sure you cannot,' the friend explained to him a bit sadly.

'I will try! You'll see. I CAN reach her,' Moss declared.

Afterwards, he tried to reach her by stretching his legs and arms. But of course he couldn't. So he threw a stone to get her to move. However, it didn't touch the Moon. So he climbed a tree, to make the rocks to go higher, but it didn't help him either.

That's why he invented the flying device, spending lots of years. Even though he invented it to go to the Moon, his dream didn't come true. But don't you think that it is very amazing that the panda made the flying device because he fell in love with the Moon?

Polar fox-cat
By sparklingfish

Polar fox-cats' names are so long, some people just call them PFCs. PFCs live in Canada, in the coldest environments. They like to eat yummy bugs, juicy fruit, and big fish. These animals can transform into different animals, such as a bowtie birds, skunky things, and BOBs. They can run faster than a cheetah, and they are the same size as most wolves you see today. If you are really really lucky, you can see one of these creatures fight a wolf over a den, or food. Obviously, the PFC wins most of the time, and the wolf runs away.

Night Zookeeper uses storytelling
and technology to encourage creativity and
imagination. Our magical stories inspire
traditional creative play and develop reading,
writing, and drawing skills.

We believe in fairness and offer free
digital education products to all children
around the world.

Thank you for buying this book
and supporting our mission.

Visit **nightzookeeper.com**
for more information.

The adventure
continues in ...

NIGHT ZOO KEEPER

The Elephant of Tusk Temple

Chapter One

Will Rivers, the Night Zookeeper, emerged on the other side of the magic portal. His friends Riya and Sam the Spying Giraffe appeared next to him. Will glanced back over his shoulder at the closing portal. He gave a final wave to the animals of Igloo City. He was going to miss Professor Penguin and Eek the Eskimouse, but Maji the elephant had told them to hurry to this new part of the Night Zoo. Will turned to face the large, lush garden in front of them.

'Aaaahh, that's better,' said Sam. He wiggled his feet in the soft grass and sighed with pleasure. 'I can feel my hooves again.'

Will unbuttoned his zookeeper's coat. He too was relieved to leave the cold behind. He drew a deep breath in through his nose. The air was warm and sweet-smelling. 'You're right, Sam,' he said. 'What a beautiful place.'

The three friends were standing on a grassy path that stretched away in front of them. There were box hedges like green walls to their left and right. Even Sam wasn't quite tall enough to see over the tops of the hedges. There were long, neat beds full of glowing, colourful flowers along the foot of each hedge. The intoxicating scent from the flowers filled their nostrils.

Riya nodded in approval. 'Wow! Do you think we've come somewhere that isn't full of danger for a change?' she asked with a wry smile.

'Oh, yes, I think so,' replied Sam with a contented yawn. 'Look. There it is: Tusk Temple.'

Will and Riya looked straight ahead down the long grassy path. Way in the distance, part of a huge purple building was visible over the top of the hedges. Two enormous columns like curved white tusks supported a roof that was shaped like an elephant's enormous forehead and ears. In the centre of the temple front was a large, glowing symbol.

Riya said, 'It's the infinity symbol, Will. That must be Maji's home.'

Will grinned. She was right. The glowing shape was just like the one he had painted on the wall of the zoo. It was just like the one he drew with his torch to make the portals. 'Well, guys, what are we waiting for? Maji told us to meet her there,' said Will. 'Let's go!'

'And at least we know the way,' said Riya with a smile. 'Not much choice this time. Straight on it is.'

Will and Riya set off along the path at a trot. A few seconds later, Will noticed Sam wasn't with them. He stopped and turned around. Sam was standing with his front legs far apart and his neck and head lowered close to the ground. He was examining one of the flower beds with so much interest that he had been left behind.

'Hey, Sam, what are you doing?' Will called back.

'Yeah, come on, Sam, Maji told us to hurry,' said Riya.

Sam turned his head to face them. 'But these flowers are amazing, even for the Night Zoo,' he replied. 'Please, just have a look.'

Will shrugged his shoulders at Riya. 'I guess a few minutes won't hurt,' he said. 'Let's see what he's found.'

Riya rolled her eyes. 'That giraffe has got you wrapped around his hoof,' she replied.

Will and Riya walked back to the stooping giraffe. They knelt beside him and looked at the luscious bed. A huge variety of flowers glowed in the soil, casting a rainbow of colours across their faces. There were flowers shaped like giant ice-cream cones, flaming tongues of fire, perfect crystal spheres and luminous feathery wings. The three friends fell silent for a few seconds, mesmerised by the spectacular sight.

Sam broke the silence, 'Each one has a name, see. They're all labelled.' Will and Riya noticed a small plaque at the base of each plant. Will read some of the labels out loud, 'Fire Tulip . . . Wings of Paradise . . . Singing Rose . . . Violent Violet . . . '

Sam's eyes flew open. 'Violent Violet!' he repeated.

Riya frowned. 'Hmmm, maybe we shouldn't get too close.'

'Yeah, come on, we'd better move on,' said Will, standing up.

Sam rose to his full height. 'Hey, Riya,' he said.

Riya looked up at him. Sam was smirking. 'Oh no,' she groaned. She knew what was coming.

'Hey, Riya, why have you got some of

those flowers on your face?' asked Sam, his dark eyes twinkling.

'Okay, I haven't got flowers on my face, but—'

'You have, you've got tulips!' chortled Sam. 'Geddit? Tulips. Two lips. Hahaha.'

Despite her best efforts, Riya giggled. 'You annoying, high-rise horse,' she said and gave him a friendly thump on the leg.

Will laughed too. The atmosphere in the garden was so calm and relaxing that he felt the tension of their other adventures slipping away. And very soon, he knew they would be with Maji in her magnificent temple and they would be safe: safe from the Voids, the army of robot spiders terrorising the Night Zoo; safe from the treacherous owl, Circles; safe from all the other dangers of the Night Zoo. Will felt a warm glow of contentment in his chest as he, Riya and Sam set off towards the temple.

'Ah, maybe this isn't going to be as simple as we thought,' said Riya.

They were facing another tall hedge. They had followed the path until they had come to a junction, where the path split left and right.

'But the temple's straight on,' complained

Sam. 'Why would you put a stupid hedge in the way?'

'Sam, can you see over the top at all?' asked Will.

'I don't think so, but I'll have a go,' said the young giraffe. He placed his feet together, stood up on the tips of his hooves and raised his long neck as high as it would go. His nostrils ended up in line with the top of the hedge, so that he could just peek over it. Sam wobbled and tottered.

'Can you see anything?' Will called up.

'Woah, it's amazing!' yelled Sam.

'Sam, stop admiring the view and tell us

what you can see,' said Riya.

'I just did!' protested Sam.

'What are you talking about? All you said was that it's amazing.'

'No, I didn't! I said it's a maze thing!'

'Oh,' said Riya. 'Right, got it. Sorry.'

'A maze?' asked Will. 'Can you see the way through to the temple?'

Sam strained his neck a few inches higher. 'No, not really, it's big and OH!' Teetering on his hooves, Sam suddenly lost balance. He stumbled to one side and then the other. Will and Riya scrambled out of the way, but there wasn't much room with the hedges blocking them in. Sam, his legs twisted beneath him, spun on the spot. His long tongue flew out of his mouth and slapped Riya in the face before he collapsed in a heap.

Riya glared at Sam. Giraffe dribble was dripping from her chin. 'Unbelievable,' she muttered.

'Come on, you two,' said Will. 'We just have to take a guess.' He looked at the two paths going in opposite directions. 'Well, left or right?'

'Left,' said Sam.

'Right,' said Riya.

Will shook his head. 'I'll choose then.'

Sometime later, the three friends stood facing another high hedge and another left-right junction. Sam was peeping over the top of the hedge.

'The temple is straight ahead of us again. We might be a bit closer now, I'm not sure.'

'Argh, this is so frustrating,' said Will. 'We seem to be going in circles!'

'I thought we'd left Circles behind in Igloo City,' said Sam with a weak smile.

They continued further into the maze, turning this way and that, away from the temple and even back on themselves, until at last they spotted something different.

'Wow, look at those,' said Sam. Ahead the path widened and on each side there were huge bushes that had been carefully cut into fantastical leafy statues.

Will approached the first one. It was a figure of an animal at least twenty feet tall. But it was like no animal he had ever seen. The top half was a rhino with a long, sharp horn but its bottom half was the powerful tail of a whale. The next plant statue had the head of a praying mantis, but the lithe body of a cheetah. There were dozens more lining the path ahead and Will, Sam and Riya wandered wide-eyed and silently amongst them.

'Hey, Sam,' said Riya. 'Here's some weird cousin of yours.' She was staring up at a beetle with a giraffe's head. 'Sam? Oh, what's he doing now?'

Will and Riya looked back at the young giraffe, who had his nose in the flowerbed again.

'What's up, Sam?' Will called back.

Sam turned to face them. He was frowning. 'I don't know. There's something funny about these bushes. My ossicones are tingling.'

'Forget it, Sam,' said Will. 'We're wasting time. Let's keep moving.' At that very moment, something moved in the flowerbed next to Sam. 'Look out!' shouted Will. A long, thick, leafy vine shot out from the bed and wrapped itself around one of Sam's front legs. Sam looked down at it in alarm and tried to pull his leg away just as another vine whipped around his other leg.

'Help me!' cried the giraffe. Will and Riya charged back towards Sam, but more vines attacked Sam with the speed of striking snakes, each one coiling itself further around the giraffe's legs, chest and neck. Sam was rooted to the spot, unable to pull away as the vines enveloped him. Riya immediately grabbed at the vines, trying to pull them off with all her strength. Will tried the same, but the vines only seemed to tighten their grip. He looked up at Sam, whose eyes were full of panic. The vine around Sam's neck was tightening so that the giraffe could only croak, 'Get them . . . off me!'

'Hang in there,' Will reassured him.

'Urgh, what are these things?' grunted Riya. She was on Sam's back yanking at a thick vine around his neck. A thought struck

Will. Yes, what were these things? He ducked down to peer into the flowerbed. The writhing vines were all coming from one plant. Will spotted the label: Silent Creeper. He glanced up at poor Sam, who was beginning to resemble one of the giant animal statues. Was it possible that all these strange creatures had been mummified by these vines? And now it was happening to Sam? Will shook the horrible thought from his mind. A Silent Creeper, he thought. How do you defeat something silent?

'Shout, Riya!' Will cried.

'What?'

'Shout! Scream, anything!'

'Okay!' Riya let go of the vines and leapt to the ground. 'Get off him! Get off!' she screamed at the top of her voice.

'Let him go!' roared Will with all his heart.

'Leave my friend alone!' screeched Riya. The vines started to quiver. The one around Sam's neck loosened and slipped down. 'It's working! Louder!' Riya encouraged them. Sam joined in, bellowing with all his might. The three of them shouted and screamed at the tops of their voices. The vines became looser and looser until they finally released Sam and retreated into the flowerbed.

'Sam, are you alright?' asked Will, hugging his friend's neck.

Sam nodded slowly. 'Thank you. That was . . . creepy!' He turned and smiled at Riya. 'You said I was your friend,' he gushed. The tip of his glistening, blue tongue popped out between his lips.

'Oh, no! Don't even think about licking me, Clumsy Longlegs,' she warned.

The Zoo Needs You!

Continue your adventure on
nightzookeeper.com

Create your own magical animals

Defeat
evil Voids

Rescue Sam the Spying Giraffe

Ready for more great stories?

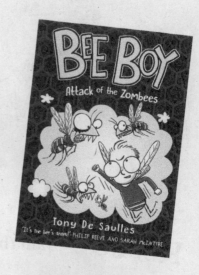